ASSASSIN

CHRIS BRADFORD

With illustrations by
Sonia Leong

In honour of three dedicated ninja,
Aidan Bracher, Matthew Maton and Charlie Harland

For more information on Chris and his books visit:

www.chrisbradford.co.uk

First published in 2014 in Great Britain by
Barrington Stoke Ltd
18 Walker Street, Edinburgh, EH3 7LP

www.barringtonstoke.co.uk

Text © 2014 Chris Bradford
Illustrations © 2014 Sonia Leong

A CIP catalogue record for this book is available
from the British Library upon request

ISBN: 978-1-78112-376-8

Printed in China by Leo

Contents

Chapter 1
Snow Patrol

Japan, Year 1580

I peer over a mound of snow. Between a gap in the trees, I spy Lord Oda.

I am Taka, a ninja – and this man, with the red scar across his cheek, is my mortal enemy.

Lord Oda sits huddled in thick blankets in a sedan chair carried by four porters. The porters struggle with their heavy burden as

they hurry down the road to the gate of Black Eagle Castle. The winter sun is setting over the mountains and the porters look nervous, in spite of the samurai soldiers that protect them.

Lord Oda's bodyguards are at the front of the line – ten warriors with the crest of a black eagle on their chests. A troop of heavily armed samurai in blood-red armour follows close behind. They wear a different crest – a roaring tiger's head. This is the emblem of Lord Kujo, the Regent of Japan.

I did not expect these samurai, and their presence here is worrying. But all I care about is that Lord Oda has at last returned home to his fortress, Black Eagle Castle. After three long months of waiting, the time has come to avenge my murdered parents.

Just as I'm about to make my move, I hear voices.

"It's so cold my eyelids are freezing together!" the first voice says.

"Stop complaining, Genzo," another man growls.

I look to my right and see a patrol of four samurai marching through the forest. I'm wearing my all-white *gi*, the ninja uniform used for winter missions, so the patrol hasn't spotted me yet ... but they are headed my way.

"Why do we have to patrol so far out from the castle?" asks the one called Genzo. He is a stick-thin man, and he hugs himself for warmth.

The leader is shivering too, but he ignores the cold as he replies. "Now our lord is back, his adviser Kenji fears a revenge attack by the ninja. So we must be on high alert. Spread out!"

The patrol splits up. Genzo passes around a snowy rock and now he is only a few paces away from me. If he keeps coming, I'm sure to be discovered.

I reach into my bag and pull out a *shuriken* – a ninja throwing star. I'm careful to hide the star's gleam from the eyes of the approaching samurai.

A pine cone drops in the snow beside my face.

I glance up. My best friend Cho is in the tree above me. Her long black hair is tucked inside her white hood and she's invisible among the snowy branches. Cho notices the *shuriken* in my hand and shakes her head at me.

Don't attack, she warns me with a glare.

But Genzo is so close I can see the dirt under his toenails. One more step and he'll be standing right on top of me.

I grip my *shuriken*, ready to leap up. I will let nothing stop me in my mission.

Chapter 2
Two Graves

Three months ago ...

I climb the steep mountain path with Cho and
Renzo, a 16-year-old boy with a shaved head
and muscles like knotted ropes.

We're almost at the top of the ridge, near
our village temple, when a voice speaks from
the darkness. "Where are you three going?" it
demands.

We spin round to see the Grandmaster of our ninja clan. He is an old man with a lined face and a long grey beard. He glares at us with eyes as pale as the moon. He is blind, but he uses his other senses to "see" the world around him.

I know that he could tell if I lied, and so I reply with the truth.

"Black Eagle Castle."

"I suppose you intend to kill Lord Oda?" the Grandmaster says. There is disapproval in his voice.

My silence is all the answer he needs.

"I expect you haven't told Tenshin," the Grandmaster says. "Our clan leader would not agree to such a mission."

"But Lord Oda has attacked our village and killed half our clan!" I protest. "Surely, he deserves to die?"

By way of reply, the Grandmaster points to the graveyard beside the temple. Four rows of new graves mark the ninja who were lost in the battle the day before. A shovel still sticks out of a pile of earth.

The Grandmaster speaks in a solemn tone. "A wise man once said – before you embark on a journey of revenge, dig two graves," he says. "One for your enemy and one for yourself."

"But we won't fail," I reply. I sound more confident than I really feel.

The Grandmaster gives a sorry shake of his head. "You misunderstand, Taka. Revenge cannot heal the hurts of the heart any more than salt water can quench thirst."

"But Lord Oda murdered my father ... and now my mother too," I cry. "I want justice!"

"Your mother Akemi protected you so that you could live on," the Grandmaster says. "She was a healer. She wouldn't want you to risk your life in a hunt for revenge."

"But I'm a ninja," I remind him. "You made me a Black Belt, you even showed me the Death Touch. Why teach me those skills if you don't want me to be an assassin?"

"I'm teaching you how to be a spy and defend yourself, not to be a cold-blooded killer," is the Grandmaster's stern reply. He looks at each of us in turn. "None of you has completed your training – you know so little of the world beyond this valley."

"That may be true, but together we're stronger than one ninja alone," says Renzo. He clasps me and Cho between his meaty arms.

"And we made a battle-bond," Cho explains. She clenches her fist and bumps it against mine.

The Grandmaster sighs. "I suppose that in order to see the light you must risk the dark. And I sense that I can't persuade you from this path. I also accept that a battle-bond cannot be broken. Wait here."

The Grandmaster limps off into the temple, and it is clear that the wounds from yesterday's battle are still raw. He returns with a small pouch, a short length of bamboo and a chain with heavy weights at each end.

"Cho, this is for you," says the Grandmaster. He hands her the bamboo and some feathered darts. "Your name means 'butterfly', but this will help you sting like a bee."

"A blowpipe." Cho grins as she inspects the hollow bamboo tube.

"It's not a toy!" the Grandmaster warns her. "Be very careful with the darts. They're tipped with poison that will knock a man out."

Cho bows her thanks. Then she slips the blowpipe and darts into her backpack, beside her double-edged sword.

The Grandmaster presents Renzo with the weighted chain. "This *manriki* weapon is made of steel and is strong like you," he says. "Use it to protect your friends."

"A Ten Thousand Power Chain!" Renzo exclaims. He whips one end of the chain through the air. It whizzes like a mad wasp. "I've always wanted one of these."

The Grandmaster turns to me. "Since you're blind to my wisdom, Taka, I give you this to disable your enemy in a fight."

"Thank you," I reply with respect. I take the pouch of fine-ground blinding powder and attach it to my belt.

"Do not think these weapons mean that I bless your mission," the Grandmaster says. "You will need more than luck to succeed."

For a moment, his words make me question my decision to hunt Lord Oda. But then I think of my mother dying in battle under that samurai's sword and I realise I've no choice in the matter.

I bow farewell to the Grandmaster, then I head up the mountain path with Cho and Renzo.

Before we disappear over the top, the Grandmaster calls after us. "I'll wait for you here and pray for your safe return. Remember our clan's motto:

When you hide, stay still as a shadow.
When you appear, strike like lightning!"

Chapter 3
Invisible

The samurai Genzo stops on the mound of snow and looks around the silent forest.

As I prepare to leap up, I recall the Grandmaster's words from three months ago. *When you appear, strike like lightning ...*

"We're wasting our time," Genzo grumbles. "There's no one out here."

The patrol leader stomps his feet to keep warm as he scans the empty landscape again.

"You're right," he says. "And it'll be dark soon. Any ninja crazy enough to be out here will freeze to death by morning."

The patrol turns back and heads towards the castle.

When I'm certain the samurai are gone, I rise up from behind the mound. Cho drops down from her hiding place in the tree.

"What were you thinking?" she whispers. "If you'd attacked that samurai, we would have had to kill them all. And a missing patrol would alert Lord Oda to the fact that we are here."

I know Cho is right. But after waiting so long for my enemy to return home, I'm impatient to get on with the mission.

"He was getting too close," I say, by way of an excuse.

"You can say that again," a rock near by agrees. "He walked right past me."

Renzo uncurls himself and snow tumbles off his broad back as he loses his boulder shape.

One of the secret arts of the ninja is to be *invisible*. As the Grandmaster once explained, this isn't the same as disappearing. It means learning how to hide in plain sight. You can climb a tree, since people rarely look up. Or stand in a field like a scarecrow. You can disguise yourself as a samurai, a monk or even a geisha girl. You can use camouflage to blend into the surroundings or change your body shape as Renzo had.

"That samurai wouldn't have spotted a pink-bottomed monkey in a kimono!" says Cho. "He was cold and wanted to get back to a warm fire."

"Well, no harm's been done," Renzo says, as he gives me a friendly slap on the back.

17

"Not yet anyway," he adds, with a look in the direction of Lord Oda's castle.

Renzo used to be my arch rival among the clan. But then I saved his life in battle, and he volunteered to join me and Cho on the mission. Not that Cho was very happy about it. She doesn't trust him ... and I suppose I shouldn't either.

"Let's make a move," Cho says. "We need to be in position before night falls."

We head to the cliff that overlooks Black Eagle Castle. This was the route Cho and I took the first time we sneaked into the fortress to steal back our clan's ninja Scrolls.

But there is a problem.

Now that Lord Oda has returned, there are double the number of sentries around the castle, and samurai are stood at the base of the cliff.

"Should we wait a few more days until they relax their guard?" Cho suggests.

"No," says Renzo. "We should enter while they're still settling down."

Cho shoots him an annoyed look. "But our plan didn't take account of the Regent's samurai that came in with Lord Oda!"

"All the more reason to go in now before they learn the layout of the castle," Renzo answers back.

Cho is about to reply, but I hold up my hand to stop them arguing. For the past three months, they've disagreed on everything, from tactics to weapons to food.

"Both of you are right," I tell them. "But we've waited long enough. We kill Lord Oda *tonight*."

Chapter 4
Ice River

We hide in the tree-line while we wait for yet another samurai patrol to pass. Because of the guards at the bottom of the cliff, we've had to change our plan and make our approach along the gorge. The route is risky, since it's so open, and we must cross the river. But we've no other option.

Before we leave the forest, we attach wooden soles to our *tabi* boots.

"Ready?" I ask.

Cho and Renzo nod.

As soon as the patrol is out of sight, we sprint across open ground.

I snatch a look back at our footprints in the snow. No samurai will ever know that we've passed this way. During our months of waiting for Lord Oda to return home, Cho carved three pairs of *ashiaro*, wooden animal footprints. With these on our feet, all we leave behind are the tracks of a fox, a deer and a dog.

The freezing night air chills my lungs as we run to the edge of the gorge. In the distance I can just see the sentries in the castle watchtowers. But the moonless night and our white *gi* make it impossible to spot us against the snow.

We reach the gorge unseen. The drawbridge has been raised. But we expected that. We take off the *ashiaro* and clamber down the rock face to the river below.

The stone is cold and slippery. My fingers become numb within seconds. I hold on as tight as I can. But one false move and I'll plummet to the rocks far below.

At last, my feet touch down on the river bank and I let out a sigh of relief.

At the bottom, we discover that luck is on our side. The river has iced over.

I throw a stone onto the crisp white surface of the ice. The stone bounces and skitters. Next, I test its strength with my weight. The ice holds and appears to be solid ... near the bank, at least.

Cho offers to go first. She skims across with no problems.

I follow, sliding my feet so as to keep my balance. As I reach the middle of the river, the ice creaks and groans beneath me. A tiny crack appears in its surface. I slide faster, praying that I'll get across in time.

With a final burst of speed, I reach the other side.

Now it's Renzo's turn. He places a foot on the ice. Then another. With nervous steps he begins his crossing. All is going well until we hear a loud CRACK!

Renzo's eyes widen in alarm. The cracks spread through the ice like a spider's web. He starts to run. Cho and I wave our arms to urge him on.

Renzo's foot goes through the ice. He falls, but he manages to launch himself forward. He slides the last few feet to the bank and beaches himself like a sea lion.

"Full marks for style," Cho smirks.

Renzo glares up at her, then shakes his wet foot. "Taka weakened the ice, that's all," he grumbles.

"Let's hope no one heard the ice break," I say.

I scan the top of the gorge for samurai. When no patrol appears, we climb up the other side. At the top, we put on our *ashiaro* again and make a final dash to the castle wall.

So far, so good.

We stay in the shadows as we creep along the base to our chosen entry point. The gates are heavily guarded and the battlements are crawling with samurai, but last month Cho spotted a row of stone-dropping holes in the eastern tower.

"There's our way in," she whispers. She points above our heads. "The holes are blocked by hatches, but we can cut our way through –"

All of a sudden, Renzo grabs Cho's arm and pulls her backwards. "Watch out!" he hisses.

Cho and I look down. The vicious teeth of a steel man-trap peek out from the snow's surface.

Cho shrugs Renzo off. "Don't worry, I saw it," she replies, as she steps around the deadly trap.

But this is a terrible mistake. Her foot triggers a second hidden trap.

Chapter 5
Wounded

The steel jaws of the trap clamp shut on Cho's leg. Her eyes flare wide in shock and terror. But she doesn't scream. She just bites hard on her hand, and lets out the softest of whimpers. Even in her agony, she knows any cry could alert the sentries.

I drop to my knees and try to pull the trap apart. But the jaws won't budge. Blood is gushing from the wound where the teeth have bitten into Cho's flesh.

Renzo grabs hold of the man-trap too. He grits his teeth and pulls at the jaws. But the spring is strong. Renzo can't open the trap wide enough to get Cho's leg out.

Cho is close to passing out with pain.

Renzo strains his muscles as he makes one last superhuman effort to free her. The jaws part a little ... then a little more.

As soon as the jagged teeth are clear of Cho's flesh, I pull her leg out. Renzo lets go and the jaws snap shut again like the bite of a hungry shark.

Cho lies in the snow. "Th ... thank you ... Renzo," she moans.

"No problem," Renzo replies, "but you owe me one."

I grab my mother's medicine kit from my pack and smother Cho's cuts in a thick green paste.

"This will stop the bleeding and numb the pain," I explain.

Cho nods as I wrap her leg in a white bandage.

Renzo scans for patrols. "We should abort the mission," he says.

"No!" Cho gasps. "We can't turn back now."

"But you're hurt," I say. "I'm not leaving you here."

"And I'm not carrying you," Renzo grunts.

"You don't need to!" Cho replies. She struggles to her feet and tests her leg. "Akemi's medicine is already working."

I check Cho's leg with concern. "Are you really fit to go on?"

Cho nods. "I just need Renzo to throw up my grappling line."

I look Cho in the eyes. "I've already lost my mother," I whisper. "I don't want to lose you too."

She clenches her fist and raises it to me. "We made a battle-bond, remember? I'm in this till the end!"

We bump fists. "You're a true ninja," I say.

Renzo launches Cho's grappling line up the tower. The hook catches on the wall above. Renzo tests it with his weight. "We're good to go," he says.

I kick fresh snow over the man-trap and patches of blood. We must hide the fact that we have been here ... and escaped the trap.

Hand over hand, we begin to climb the castle wall. In spite of her hurt leg, Cho pulls herself up the rope with the ease of a spider. Renzo and I wear *shuko* hand-claws to climb the sheer rock face.

We reach the stone-dropping holes. I cut the leather fastenings of a wooden hatch with my knife. When I peer in the open hole, I see a guard-room with a fire blazing in the grate. Next to the fire there is a large pile of rocks, ready to repel any attack.

The room appears to be empty.

Silently I clamber through the hole, followed by Cho and Renzo. We head over to the far door. But as we pass the rock pile, we come face to face with a samurai guard.

Chapter 6
Stealth, Not Strength

The samurai is slumbering by the fire. I exchange uneasy glances with Cho and Renzo. The guard is a huge brute of a man with a bushy beard, but his eyes remain closed.

We creep across the room. The only noise is the snap and crackle of the fire.

Cho is almost at the door when I'm grabbed from behind and flung across the room. I crash head-first into the pile of rocks. I am stunned by the impact, and I can only watch as the bearded samurai swings a massive fist at Renzo.

Renzo ducks just in time and counters with a brutal punch to the samurai's gut. The strike would floor an ox, but the samurai doesn't seem to feel it. Renzo tries again, this time with a hook punch to the jaw. This time the samurai just laughs.

"You'll need to hit me harder than that, young ninja!" he says.

The samurai seizes Renzo by the throat and lifts him off the ground. As Renzo struggles in the samurai's grip, he starts choking to death.

Then, without warning, the samurai collapses to the floor.

Cho stands behind him, a blowpipe dart in her hand. "As the Grandmaster once said,

why punch a rock when you can pierce a plum?"
she says.

Renzo rubs his throat. "Thanks," he rasps.

"Now we're even," Cho says.

I get to my feet too. My head throbs from
where it hit the rock pile, and I sway a little
as I walk over to Renzo. Together we drag the
samurai out of sight behind the rocks. He is
still out cold. Then we leave the guard-room
and hurry down a set of stone steps into an
outer courtyard.

The crunch of marching feet alerts us
to a patrol. We dive into the doorway of
a storehouse just as a unit of the Regent's
samurai strides by. The samurai enter an
inner gateway. They ignore the two sentries
who open the gate for them.

As the patrol disappears, one of the sentries
begins to complain. "Who do they think they

are? Marching around as if they own the place."

The other sentry shakes his head in disgust. "They soon might. I hear the Regent is sending his entire army to wipe out the ninja."

The first sentry smiles. "Good. It's time we got rid of those scum. They're nothing but trouble."

When he hears this, Renzo takes out his *manriki* chain. But I stop him before he can swing it.

"Stealth, not strength," I whisper.

I pick a pebble up off the ground and toss it to the far side of the courtyard. It hits a wall and clatters down a set of steps.

"Did you hear that?" says the first sentry. He peers into the darkness.

The other sentry nods. "I suppose we'd better take a look," he sighs. "Kenji ordered us to check out everything."

As they leave their posts, we sprint across to the gate. Cho tries the handle, but it won't turn. I take out my smallest *shuriken* and try to pick the lock with the thin spike.

"Hurry," Cho urges. "I can hear them coming back."

The footsteps in the snow get closer and closer.

In my rush, I drop the spike. As I scramble to pick it up, Renzo tries the gate handle himself. With a firm push, the latch clicks open.

Renzo smirks at Cho. "It just needed a little strength!"

Chapter 7

Blood in the Snow

We dart through the gate and close it behind us. The main tower of Black Eagle Castle looms over us as we cross an inner courtyard. We know from our last mission here that Lord Oda's rooms are on the third floor.

Renzo stops beside a high wall, leans against it and cups his hands. I put my foot into them and he boosts me over. I somersault through the air and land in a garden on the other side. There's a pond surrounded by stone lanterns, bushes and a cherry-blossom tree.

As Cho drops down next to me, she lets out a gasp of pain. I see that her bandage is seeping blood.

"Are you all right?" I whisper.

"I'm fine," she says. She limps across the snow-covered garden towards the tower. Her lips are clamped.

As I go to follow her, a short bald man with a round belly enters the garden. Cho disappears into the bushes, but I'm caught out in the open.

I freeze where I am. I don't even blink.

As the man strolls along the garden path, I recognise him. He is Lord Oda's adviser, Kenji. He looks straight at me ... then smiles.

"Ah! The gardener's made a snowman." He chuckles. "But it needs a nose."

As Kenji bends down to take a pebble from the path, he catches sight of a patch of blood in the snow. His eyes follow the red trail to the bushes.

Kenji realises the danger and goes to cry out. "NIN –"

A dart pierces his neck and the word dies in his throat. Kenji collapses face-first in the snow.

Renzo lands beside me, silent as a leopard.

"Talk about hiding in plain sight," he laughs.

I nod in agreement. "I don't think even the Grandmaster will believe it!"

Renzo helps me pull Kenji behind the cherry-blossom tree. Then he kicks the tree trunk and the adviser is buried in a shower of snow.

"Sweet dreams, samurai," Renzo laughs.

Cho limps out of the bushes, with her blowpipe in her hand. While Renzo covers the blood trail, I tie a new bandage around her leg. She looks at the lumpy snow mound under the tree.

"We'd better move fast," she says. "It won't be long before someone realises he's missing."

Chapter 8
Nightingale Floor

We scale the main tower and enter by an open window on the third floor. The outer corridor is lit by oil lamps, but there's enough darkness for us to keep to the shadows.

We avoid a pair of samurai guards, then sneak around until we come to a long hallway that ends in a grand door. The door is decorated with a black eagle on top of a golden mountain.

"This must be Lord Oda's room," I whisper.

Cho stares down the hallway. "But why are there no guards?" she asks.

"They're probably on the other side," Renzo replies.

We're about to make our approach when the door slides open and a serving girl appears. I spot at least two of Lord Oda's bodyguards in the next room.

We retreat further into the shadows and watch as the serving girl shuffles down the hallway. I can hear the sound of birds chirping with her every step.

"*Uguisubari!*" Cho gasps, when the serving girl has gone. "A Nightingale Floor!"

Renzo and I look at her, confused.

"The Grandmaster once told me about these anti-assassin floors," she explains. "They're almost impossible to walk on without making a noise and alerting the guards."

"So how do we get across?" Renzo asks.

"*Uki-ashi*," Cho replies.

I shake my head in dismay. "Floating Feet! I haven't practised that type of stealth walk in ages."

"Well, this is as good a time as any," Cho says.

Even with her wounded leg, Cho glides across the Nightingale Floor as silently as a ghost. Her feet don't even seem to touch the wooden boards.

Once Cho has reached the door, Renzo moves next. He's far heavier than me, but has had two more years of ninja training. He

is slower than Cho, but he crosses the floor without making it "sing" out.

Now it's my turn. I imagine myself as light as a feather and place my toes on the edge of the first floorboard. I move my feet in a circular fashion and inch forwards. I never let my weight rest too long on one spot because that would trigger the Nightingale Floor.

I feel a bead of sweat run down my brow as I glide across. I need all my focus to "float" my feet. Each floorboard is a new challenge. I have to sense its shape, where the danger spots are. I cannot pause for one second.

I'm nearly there ... two more boards to go ...

But then I rush my last step and the sound of a nightingale breaks the silence.

Chapter 9

Bodyguards

A bodyguard opens the door and peers down the hallway.

"No one's there," he says to another guard.

I can see the top of the man's shaved head and I pray he doesn't look up. My arms shake as I hold myself between the wooden beams of the ceiling.

Renzo and Cho are next to me, and we are all trembling with the effort of keeping ourselves up.

"Must have been that serving girl," the bodyguard says, and he slides the door shut.

With relief, we silently lower ourselves to the ground. Cho takes out her blowpipe and signals to me to get a *shuriken*. Renzo understands her plan, and he puts his fingers to the door and slides it open a crack. Cho slips the end of her blowpipe through ...

Phut!

The dart flies across the room and strikes the first bodyguard. As he collapses to the floor, Renzo flings open the door and I throw my *shuriken* at the second bodyguard. Before the man can cry out a warning, the ninja star hits him in the throat. He slumps down beside his partner.

Now that we're in Lord Oda's private rooms, we have to move fast. Surprise is everything in an attack. I run to the opposite door and peek through to an inner chamber. The floor is covered with *tatami* straw mats. The paper walls are decorated with images of hunting birds – falcons, hawks and eagles.

This chamber is deserted, but a candle burns bright in the next room. Its glow casts the shadow of a kneeling man upon the other side of the paper wall.

"I think I see him!" I hiss. I take out the poisoned *shuriken* I've saved for my enemy.

Cho looks around the empty chamber. "This is too easy," she says.

But my eagerness gets the better of me.

I start to stealth walk across the room. I pass a painting of a blue-black falcon ... then a swooping hawk ... then, all of a sudden, a painting of a golden eagle opens up and two bodyguards charge into the room.

Other panels spin open and six more guards appear, with their swords drawn.

Cho pulls out her own sword just in time to block an attempt to behead her. Renzo whips out his *manriki*.

"GO, TAKA!" Renzo cries, as he knocks out a samurai with the weight on one end of his chain. "We'll hold them off!"

I leap aside to avoid a cruel slice from a bodyguard's sword. The tip of the blade just misses me, but it cuts into my bag. All my *shuriken* scatter across the floor.

I flick my last *shuriken* – the one meant for Lord Oda – at the bodyguard's right arm. It pierces his bicep and he drops his sword. The devastating side-kick I give him sends him flying through the paper wall into the next room.

On the other side of the ripped hole I see the scarred face of Lord Oda.

Chapter 10
Broken Heart

I step over the body of the guard and enter the room.

Lord Oda sits upon a raised platform, where he watches me without fear as I approach. In front of him is a short sword. But he makes no attempt to reach for it.

Now I have no *shuriken* left, I must get close enough to use the Death Touch. But this time Lord Oda won't survive the attack. For now I know where his heart really lies. Not on the left side of his body, like a normal man. But on the right.

"I knew you'd come," Lord Oda says. "You really are your father's son."

"You *murdered* my father!" I say. I feel my blood boil – although I was only a baby at the time and have no memory of it.

Lord Oda shakes his head. "That's not true."

"*How can you say that?*" I cry. "You killed my mother too."

"And I have suffered ever since that day," Lord Oda replies. His voice is heavy with sorrow.

The remorse that he claims makes me even angrier. Three months have passed since the battle to save our village, but I can still remember, clear as day, the moment Lord Oda thrust his blade into my mother.

I take another step forward and look at the sword lying between us. "Aren't you going to defend yourself?" I say.

"This sword isn't for you," replies Lord Oda. "It's for me to –"

Before Lord Oda can trick me with his words, I grab the sword to strike him down dead.

"I deserve to die," Lord Oda says, and he bows his head in surrender. "For I killed the woman I loved."

I stop the blade in mid-air. "Wh … what?"

"Akemi. Your mother." He looks up at me and his eyes are red with tears. "Fifteen years ago, when I was a young samurai and not yet a lord, I met Akemi while I was out hunting in the

mountains. Over that summer, we fell in love. At the time I had no idea your mother was a ninja. And, to be honest, I wouldn't have cared."

I stand stock still. I can't believe my ears. But the truth is clear to read in the grief on Lord Oda's face. He means every word.

"Then why?" I ask. "If you were so in love with my mother, why do you want to destroy our ninja clan?"

"Because your clan leader destroyed our love!" Lord Oda snarls.

Anger flashes in his eyes and I take a step back.

"See this scar?" Lord Oda points to the red line that cuts across his right cheek. "Your old clan leader sent Akemi to kill the son of the new Lord of Black Eagle Castle. She had no idea that son was me. We fought in the dark, and her knife slashed my face. Then a shaft of moonlight let us see one another ..."

Lord Oda trembles, as if he is haunted by the memory.

"We ... we cried in each other's arms at our tragic fate ... Akemi was faced with an impossible choice – me or the clan."

Lord Oda becomes choked with emotion and cannot speak. But his expression tells me more than he could ever say.

At last he manages to go on. "Your mother may not have killed me that night ... but she broke my heart. But I don't blame her. I blame the clan – and I always will."

Lord Oda looks at me, a sad yet tender smile on his face. "As Akemi died I heard her call your name. I couldn't believe it! We were going to call our first-born son ... Taka."

Chapter 11
Father

I drop the sword in shock. "You lie! I'm not your son."

"I *know* you are," Lord Oda replies. "How old are you now? Fourteen?"

I want to deny the truth. "I'm no samurai," I shout. "I'm a ninja!"

"You're both," he says with a short laugh. "Akemi's son the ninja. My son the samurai."

"But *you* murdered my father at the Battle of Black Eagle Castle."

"No, I killed your old clan leader. Your real father never died in that battle. But the night Akemi was sent to kill me, he did die *here*." Lord Oda points to where his heart is. "What was left turned rotten and hateful. But now I've lived to see you, my son, there is some light in the darkness."

I am stunned by all of this, frozen to the spot. The sword lies at my feet, still within reach. *Yet how can I kill my own father?*

Angry shouts and alarm bells sound all over the castle.

Cho staggers into the room. "They must have found Kenji!" she cries. There is blood splattered across her white *gi*.

Renzo follows behind, a deep gash on his head. He stares at the samurai lord in amazement. "Why haven't you killed him yet?" he demands.

I turn to my friends. "I can't ... He's my father," I say.

Cho and Renzo are shocked into silence. Footsteps thunder up the castle's wooden stairs.

"You must go!" Lord Oda urges.

"If you're his father," Cho says, "then you can stop them."

Lord Oda shakes his head. "They're not my men to command," he replies. "The Regent's samurai are here for one purpose only – to wipe out every ninja in the land. But I can help you escape."

Lord Oda opens a wall panel to reveal a secret passage.

"This leads to the main gatehouse," he says. "Now go."

I have no choice but to trust Lord Oda. I duck into the passage with Cho and Renzo.

"Here, take this," says Lord Oda, and he hands me a scroll. "These are the plans for the Regent's attack. I've had a change of heart – use them to save your clan."

"Thank you ... Father."

Lord Oda smiles as if for the last time. "Goodbye, my son."

Chapter 12
Drawbridge

We exit the passage into the winch room of the castle.

Cho can barely walk. The fight with the bodyguards has taken its toll on her.

"Let me help you," I say, and I put an arm round her waist.

She's too weak to protest.

Renzo heads over to the winch, releases the catch and lowers the drawbridge.

The door bursts open and a samurai guard appears. "No one ordered the bridge to be –" He stops as his eyes widen in amazement at the sight of three blood-stained ninja.

The samurai draws his sword and charges at Renzo.

I reach into the pouch on my belt and throw the blinding powder into the man's eyes. He reels backwards, straight into the winch. One of its spinning handles smashes him on the head and he collapses to the floor.

"Time to go!" I say, as Renzo helps me to support Cho.

We stagger onto the drawbridge. In the courtyard behind, a unit of the Regent's samurai spots us.

"After them!" their leader orders.

The samurai rush towards us and they are fast gaining ground.

"You take Cho," Renzo says.

"But what about you?" I say.

"We made a battle-bond," he replies, holding up a clenched fist. "You saved my life. Now it's my turn to save yours."

Renzo bumps his fist against mine, then turns to face the enemy.

"GO!" he shouts.

I carry Cho across the bridge and we stumble towards the forest. Behind us, I can hear the wasp buzz of Renzo's *manriki*.

"WHO'S FIRST?" he roars at the Regent's samurai.

As we reach the edge of the forest, I hear a scream as someone falls into the gorge.

I look back in fear for Renzo. But he's still standing on the bridge, battling the samurai. That's the last I see of my brave and loyal friend.

Chapter 13
In the Shadows

The fire crackles in the hearth of the Grandmaster's temple. Cho and I warm ourselves by its heat. Her leg rests on a cushion, and there are fresh bandages round her wound. She sips from a bowl of herb soup that the Grandmaster has made. She already looks much better.

"So, it seems that Lord Oda *is* my father," I say, once I have told the Grandmaster the whole story.

The Grandmaster nods. "Now I understand why Akemi refused to go on any more missions and became a healer instead."

I hand him the scroll that my father gave me. The Grandmaster examines its wax seal with his fingertips.

"This is the true seal of the Regent!" the Grandmaster says in surprise. "These battle plans might just save the clan."

"We paid a heavy price for them," Cho says, and a tear rolls down her cheek.

We all bow our heads in honour of Renzo, who gave up his life for us.

Then I turn to the Grandmaster. "Instead of always fighting, why can't there be a truce between ninja and samurai?" I ask.

The Grandmaster shakes his head. "The ninja and the samurai are as opposite as the moon and the sun," he explains. "Just as night can never share the day, so the ninja will never be accepted by the samurai. But we will survive. For the ninja live in the shadows."

Suddenly, a shivering youth steps out of the darkness.

"Renzo!" we exclaim in amazement and joy.

"Sorry I'm late," Renzo says, and he collapses by the fire.

I raise my fist in salute. Cho does the same, and we all bump fists.

"To living in the shadows!" I say.

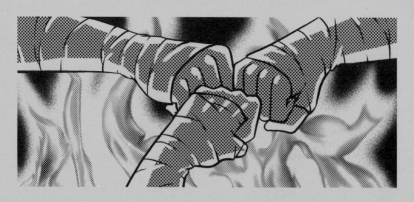